Dracula's
DE-COMPOSITION
BOOK

Other books by Holly Kowitt:

This Book Is a Joke

Off-the-Hook Big Book of Really Dumb School Jokes

99 $^{1}/_{2}$ Animal Jokes

99 $^{1}/_{2}$ Gross Jokes

99 $^{1}/_{2}$ Scary Jokes

Dracula's
DE-COMPOSITION BOOK

by Holly Kowitt

SCHOLASTIC INC.

New York Toronto London Auckland Sydney
Mexico City New Delhi Hong Kong Buenos Aires

ISBN-13: 978-0-545-00307-0

ISBN-10: 0-545-00307-5

12 11 10 9 8 7 6 5 4 3 2 1   7 8 9 10 11 12/0

40

Printed in the U.S.A.

First Printing, September 2007

To Godzilla,
Frankenstein,
the Blob,
and David Manis —
This is dead-icated

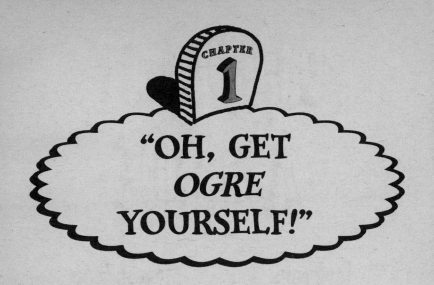

"OH, GET OGRE YOURSELF!"

What's Dracula's favorite holiday?
St. Batrick's Day

What inning is it when Frankenstein plays shortstop?
The frightinning

How does the Cyclops listen to music?
On an Eye-pod

**Why did Godzilla destroy a pay phone
at the football stadium?**
He was trying to get the quarterback.

DRACULA AT A GLANCE

fave car:
Necks-us

Biggest fear:
Tooth decay

fave fruit:
Adam's apple

Likes to attend:
Bat Mitzvahs

fave animal:
Giraffe

favorite town:
Great Neck, New York

Quote:
"DOES this cape make
me look fat?"

TOP 10

REASONS WHY I, DRACULA, LOVE BLOOD

10. It's delicious

9. Coffee keeps me awake all day

8. It's thicker than water — and tastes better

7. Doesn't stain red upholstery

6. Great on fries

5. Bloodatarian restaurants are never crowded

4. Comes in Chunky Gardenstyle

3. Ever hear of a Red Cross soda drive?

2. Enjoy playing Follow the Liter

1. Root beer makes me burp

Werewolf AT A GLANCE

fave clothing:
Roc-a-Werewolf

fave store:
Beast Buy

fave author:
J. K. Howling

fave TV:
Anything on Fox

fave airport:
O'Hair

Hopes to attend:
Claw school

Quote:
"anyone seen my five-speed back shaver?"

What's as sharp as a vampire's fang?
The other fang

What do you do when fifty vampires show up at your house?
Hope it's Halloween

Where do you store a werewolf?
In a were-house

How did Dracula's victim feel after he left?
Gnawed so good

Why couldn't the postman deliver the mail to the witch's house?
There wasn't a zip toad.

Why does Godzilla eat hotel rooms?
He has a suite tooth.

DRACULA'S DREAM HOUSE

1. Sealy Perma-Rest coffin
2. Skeletons in closet
3. Private bloodbath
4. Bat robe
5. Beanbag chair made out of the Blob
6. Big-scream TV
7. Wreck room
8. Welcome bat
9. Take-out menu
10. Kitchen covered in (rep)tiles
11. Casketball court
12. Bloodshed

What's Dracula's favorite circus act?
He always goes for the juggler.

Why couldn't the ghost keep a secret?
He was dying to tell someone!

What do ghost firemen use?
Haunted hoses

Ghost #1: How are you feeling?
Ghost #2: Oh, all white, I guess.

**Where do ghosts sell
their stuff?**
On eeeeeeeeeeeeBay

**How does a ghost
like his hamburger?**
Medium scared

**What did the old
ghost say to the
younger one?**
"My, how you've groaned!"

**What do you get when you give
the Invisible Man a boogie board?**
Surfing like you've never seen

**What happened when Godzilla tore the
top off the department store?**
Prices went through the roof.

How does Big Foot walk around?
With bear feet

What's the Blob's favorite dance?
The garbage can-can

What do zombies call it when they dig up a body and bring it home?
Take-out

What does Godzilla put on letters?
Stomps

Why was the witch kicked out of class?
She was hex-messaging.

Who drinks blood, lives in Springfield, and has parents named Marge and Homer?
Bat Simpson

What restaurants do vampires avoid?
Stake houses

Why didn't the corpse visit friends when he started to decompose?
He felt like he was losing face.

What kind of blood type does a pessimist have?
B negative

Where do mummies deposit their money?
In the banks of the Nile

CHAPTER 2

"HEX-CUUUUUUUUUSE ME!"

Why did the ghost pick his nose?
He had boo-gers.

Why couldn't the cannibal sell his house?
He was charging an arm and a leg.

How does a monster congratulate someone?
He gives him a high six.

What position did the Blob play on the baseball team?
Scenter field

Do mummies make good skateboarders?
Yeah, they really shred.

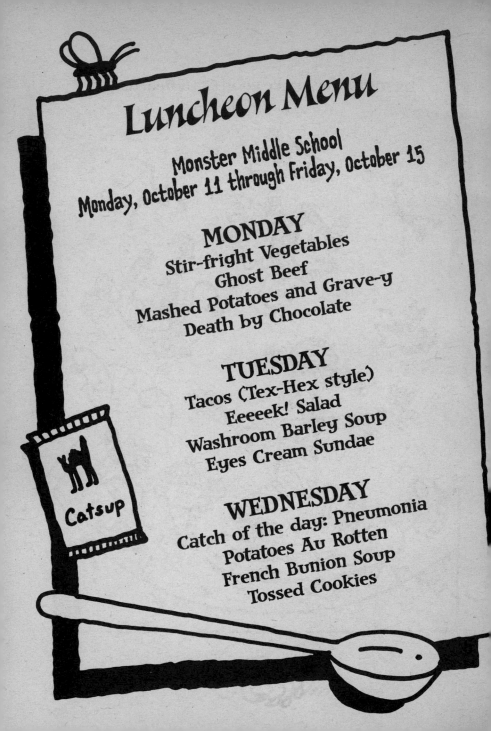

Luncheon Menu

Monster Middle School
Monday, October 11 through Friday, October 15

MONDAY
Stir-fright Vegetables
Ghost Beef
Mashed Potatoes and Grave-y
Death by Chocolate

TUESDAY
Tacos (Tex-Hex style)
Eeeeek! Salad
Washroom Barley Soup
Eyes Cream Sundae

WEDNESDAY
Catch of the day: Pneumonia
Potatoes Au Rotten
French Bunion Soup
Tossed Cookies

Catsup

THURSDAY
Pee Soup
Grilled Dork Chops
Green Beings
Slime Jello

FRIDAY
Cannibal Special:
Fish and Chip
Greens with Fresh Ginger
Tater Tots
Brownies

All meals will be served with choice of juice, milk,
or tea (decoffinated).
Remove your trays after everyone's eaten.

GODZILLA AT A GLANCE

fave drink:
Lake Michigan

Currently reading:
Twenty stories

fave TV:
Stalk shows

Dream job:
Destruction worker

Pet peeve:
Bad dubbing

Best feature:
Makes big impression

Quote:
"aRRRRRRRRRGGGGGH!"

20

MONSTER

Very attracted to positive people
(O-positive). Bat-chelor seeks
long-necked girl. U my type? 555-DRAC.

I have seven bulging eyes,
five wart-covered noses, and
twelve slobbering mouths.
Box 25.

Successful doctor likes to **make** new
friends. Franknstine@ghoulmail.

Me: At 7–11 Friday morning.
Mucous-encrusted ghoul.
You: Same, but with two heads.
Our eyes met. You held my hand.
Can I have it back?
Ghoulia@ghoulmail.

PERSONAL ADS

Rampaging giant seeks someone equally **smashing**. E-maul Godzilla@earthstink.

LOOKING FOR MR. (F)RIGHT — Tired of guys who turn out not to be creeps. Witch@broommail.

Mummy 3,000 years old but looks 2,000. Let's get together and unwind. Box 48.

INVISIBLE MAN lonely since **girlfriend stopped seeing me**. Sorry, no photo. Box 120.

Cute cannibal seeks ~~edible~~ eligible bachelors. Let's go out for **Sue-shi or Italians**. just8@boohoo.

23

THE BLOB AT A GLANCE

fave Restaurant:
Upchuck E. Cheese

fave Band:
'N Stink

fave Books:
Best smellers

fave Snack:
Stench fries

fave Activity:
Taking in the garbage

Slogan:
"Time's fun when you're having flies."

TOP 10

MONSTER TV OPTIONS

10. Good Mourning, America

9. America's Next Top Monster

8. The EEEEEEEE! Channel

7. One-Eye Witness News

6. Pay-Per-Boo

5. Hollywood Extraterrestrial

4. Lifestyles of the Witch and Famous

3. Wide World of Warts

2. America's Most Haunted

1. Extreme Make-Ogre

Mrs. Van Winkle: Wake up!
You've been asleep for twenty years!
Rip Van Winkle: Please — just five
more minutes!

**Why did the corpse bring a maggot
to the school prom?**
The invitation said he could bring a pest.

**Why was the witch kicked out of the
school cafeteria?**
She asked for bigger potions.

What's Dracula's favorite place in South Africa?
Cape Town

Did you hear about the ghost in Congress?
He's Spooker of the House.

Dragon #1: Where did you find Sir Galahad's belly button?
Dragon #2: In the middle of the knight.

What do mummies like best about football?
The post game wrap-up

Why did Dracula pull his cape over his head?
He was working undercover.

Why did the witch bring a broom to the party?
It was a sweep-over.

Why did Dracula go to his family reunion?
He likes the necks of kin.

Why couldn't the mummy come to the phone?
'Cuz he was tied up.

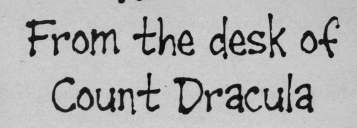

From the desk of Count Dracula

STUFF TO DO

1. Let meat go rotten

2. Speak to Godzilla about his firebreath

3. File fangs

4. See if morgue has "All You Can Eat" night

5. TiVo "Coroner's Report"

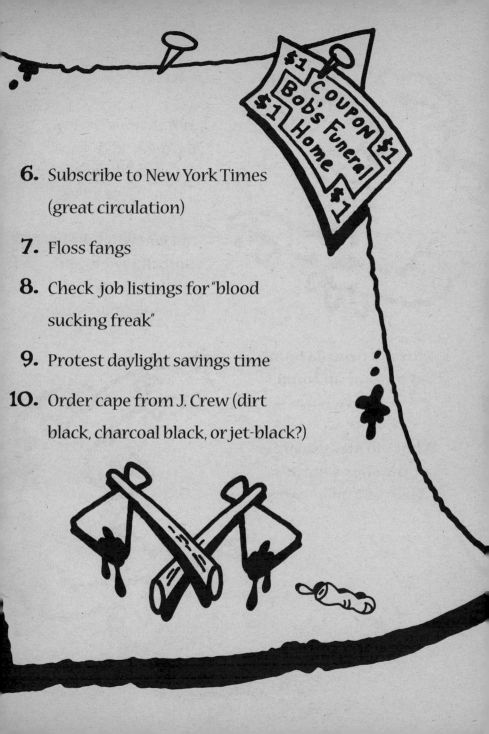

6. Subscribe to New York Times (great circulation)

7. Floss fangs

8. Check job listings for "blood sucking freak"

9. Protest daylight savings time

10. Order cape from J. Crew (dirt black, charcoal black, or jet-black?)

$1 COUPON
Bob's Funeral Home
$1 $1 $1

What's pale, wears a cape, and doesn't suck blood?
Dracula on a diet

Did you hear about Godzilla's new job?
He's a roar-to-roar salesman.

Why did Dracula bomb as a stand-up comic?
He told bat jokes.

What did Medusa order at the soda fountain?
Chocolate milk snakes

Did you hear about the new monster movie?
It's rated aaaaarrrgh.

What did one toilet monster say to another?
"Potty on, Dude!"

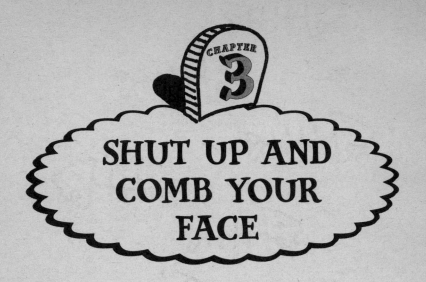

SHUT UP AND COMB YOUR FACE

Why did the monster go to LensCrafters?
He wanted new eye-eye-eyeglasses.

What does Frankenstein do in the fall?
His back to school shocking

What does Godzilla call the Twin Cities?
A convenient snack-pack

How do vampires fall asleep?
They count Draculas.

Dracula: How'd you do on that IQ test?
The Blob: It came back negative.

Why did Frankenstein ask the nurse for glue?
He had a splitting headache.

Where was the Blob educated?
Smell-ementary school

**Why does Dracula end up on
the chandelier every night?**
He's a light sleeper.

Why do werewolves have
big nostrils?

Because they have big fingers!

FRANKENSTEIN AT A GLANCE

fave lunch:
2000 volts

favorite coffee:
Scarbucks

fave subject:
Current events

fave piano:
Franken-Steinway

fave sport:
Bodybuilding

fashion look:
High collars to hide
neck bolts

Quote:
"Talk to the hand!"

What happens when you photograph the Invisible Man?

Nothing develops

Why do skeletons play the piano?
They don't have organs.

What happened to Shakespeare when he died?
He became a ghost writer.

How do ghosts stay in shape?
Scare-obics

ABOMINABLE SNOWMAN AT A GLANCE

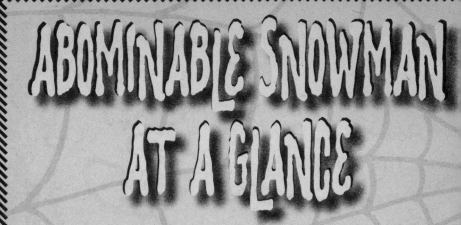

Commutes by:
Icicle

fave restaurant:
Brr-grr King

fave store:
Cold Navy

fave cereal:
Frosted Flakes

Hates:
Sitting in front
of a fire

Quote:
"Chill, dude."

TOP 10

LEAST SCARY HORROR MOVIES

10. It Came From the Gap

9. Night of the Living Quiche

8. Wednesday the 13th

7. Care Bear on Elm Street

6. The Whining

5. Aliens Gone Mild

4. Invasion of the Potty Snatchers

The day started with Mom getting on my case.

Make your coffin!

At school we had a substitute creature.

These kids are **monsters**.

Of course, I got in trouble.

No stalking out of turn!

Teachur

It went downhill from there.

Your graves are lousy.

PRINCIPAL

My best friend couldn't have lunch with me.

Band practice. Horn section.

How do you send a message to a werewolf?
Use a fox machine.

How did the monster know the cafe was out of his favorite food?
The sign on the door said NO PETS.

What do hangmen read in their spare time?
The noosepaper

Why did the family of werewolves climb onto Godzilla?
So he could have his own backpack

Why did the Thing cross the road?
He wanted some chicken for his coffee.

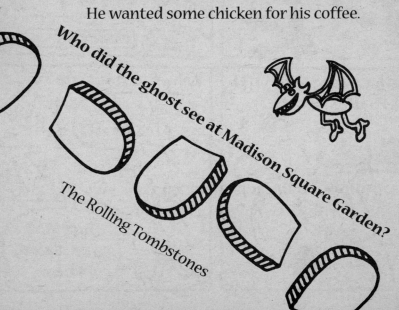

Who did the ghost see at Madison Square Garden?

The Rolling Tombstones

What did they say when the witch died playing croquet?
"Ding dong the wicket witch is dead!"

Why did Frankenstein carry a picket sign?
He heard there was a demon-stration.

What state has the most werewolves?
Dela-were

How did Dracula make his cape last?
He made the rest of his suit first.

I.M. *SO* OVER IT

MONSTERS INSTANT MESSAGE EACH OTHER:

teenzomB: u going to the dance

skeletongrrrl: mayb. u?

TZ: no body 2 go with

SG: dig someone up

TZ: who

SG: ghost boi

TZ: total airhead

SG: u seen abominable snowman

TZ: not yeti

SG: y not him

TZ: LOL. he doesn't even know im alive

SG: you're not

TZ: lunch?

SG: can't. trying 2 lose excess flesh

TZ: lets stalk l8r

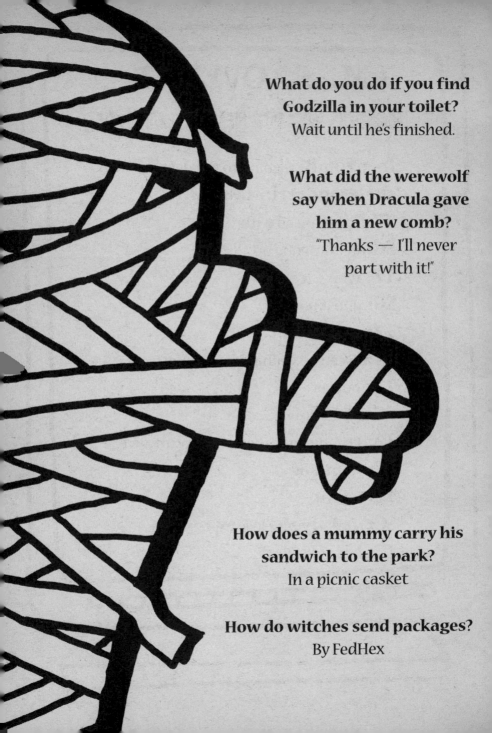

What do you do if you find Godzilla in your toilet?
Wait until he's finished.

What did the werewolf say when Dracula gave him a new comb?
"Thanks — I'll never part with it!"

How does a mummy carry his sandwich to the park?
In a picnic casket

How do witches send packages?
By FedHex

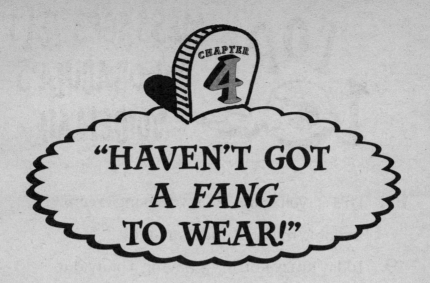

CHAPTER 4

"HAVEN'T GOT A *FANG* TO WEAR!"

Where does Godzilla buy his clothes?
At the maul

What did the executioner's ad say?
"Only Ten Chopping Days
Before Christmas!"

**Why does the monster
bowling league meet at eight?**
Because Dracula always
strikes at night.

TOP 10

MESSAGES LEFT ON DRACULA'S VOICEMAIL

10. "This is Wolfman. Got any shaving cream? I'm doing my back and I ran out."

9. "Today Krazy Koffins is having a blow-out sale. . . ."

8. "Domino's confirming your order: cockroaches, worms, anchovies — NO GARLIC."

7. "This is Blockbuster. You have a bunch of overdue Dracula movies."

6. "Dude, it's Frankenstein. Wanna go to Johnny's for ribs? Or Charlie's for lungs?"

5. "Domino's calling. Have you seen our delivery guy?"

4. "Castle Jewelers? I'm calling about your ad for a neck model."

3. "Dentist's office. Time for your yearly fang-cleaning."

2. "Domino's again. The last three delivery guys never came back!"

1. "Time to change your outgoing message, dude. It's, like, 300 years old."

TEEN WITCH AT A GLANCE

fave food:
Tex-Hex

fave pen:
Magic Markers

fave color:
Basic black

fave celeb:
Tori Spelling

Biggest perk:
Frequent Flyer Miles

Quote:
"Mom, can I have keys
to the broom tonight?"

What did Godzilla say when he gave out piggyback rides to kids?
"Dinner's on me tonight."

Who's more disgusting, the Blob or the son of a supermarket owner?
The son, because he's a little grocer.

What's a maggot's favorite phone service?
Crawl-waiting

What happened when the Blob won the lottery?
He became filthy rich.

What did the Abominable Snowman win at the Winter Olympics?
The Cold Medal

What kind of monster drives a carpool?
A mini-vanpire

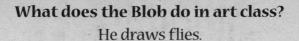

What does the Blob do in art class?
He draws flies.

What jewels do ghosts wear?
Gravestones

**Why did vultures keep returning to the
lousy restaurant?**
The food was rotten.

Where do ghosts play tennis?
On a tennis corpse

Why did Big Foot put logs in his bed?
He wanted to have a lumber party.

Why did Frankenstein drill a hole in his head?
He wanted to keep an open mind.

**Why did Dracula join
the football team?**
They needed a
quarterbat.

MUMMY AT A GLANCE

fave music:
Wrap

Travel:
Wrap-ped transit

Pet peeve:
Dry skin

future job:
Cairo-practor

State of mind:
De Nile

Common complaint:
She sphinx

Overheard remark:
"Egypt me!"

Monster Middle School Library

OVERDUE NOTICE FOR: *Count Dracula*

The following items must be returned immediately:

Books:

Nancy Drew Blood Mysteries

Magic Ghoul Bus

Are You There, Godzilla? It's Me, Margaret

The Molar Express

Ooze Who In America

Amelia Bat-elia

Rise And Fall Of The Roman Vampire

Hairy Clotter

Videos:

Planet Of The Capes

Star Trek: The Necks Generation

Count Dracula
Castle Drive #8
Transylvania
55555

Monster: Doctor, do the tests show I'm normal?
Doctor: Yes, both your heads are fine.

The Blob: Why did you tell everyone I was stupid?
Dracula: I'm sorry! I didn't know you were keeping it a secret.

Witch: Waiter, do you serve senior citizens?
Waiter: Only when we're out of everything else!

If the Blob has a stuffy nose, how does he smell?
Terrible!

**What does Godzilla eat when he goes
to the Hard Rock Café?**
The Hard Rock Café

How do you get a monster out of your backpack?
The same way you got him in.

Why did the monster go surfing?
He wanted to hang eleven.

Why did the werewolf get a job on the night shift?
He didn't want to lurk nine-to-five.

What instructor helps ghosts speak correctly?
The screech teacher

How does a witch tell time?
With a witch watch

**Why did Godzilla jump off a building
in Times Square?**
He wanted to make a hit on Broadway.

Where does Dracula buy his pencils?
Pennsylvania

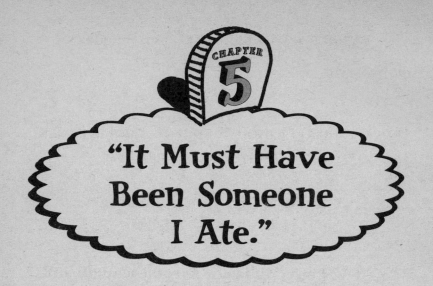

"It Must Have Been Someone I Ate."

Why did the skeleton go to the hospital?
To have his ghoul bladder out

Does anyone know if Godzilla really stepped on that boardinghouse?
Not yet, but roomers are flying.

Why was Dracula thrown out of the butcher shop?
He was chop-lifting.

What do you find on the windows of a ghost's house?
Shudders!

Abominable Snowman: I couldn't attack anyone in this blizzard.
Mrs. Abominable Snowman: That's snow excuse!

Dracula: Godzilla is a very careful driver.
The Blob: Really?
Dracula: Yes, he always looks both ways before hitting something.

Why don't zombies have money problems?
They never worry about the cost of living.

Why did Frankenstein buy a vegetable stand?
He wanted to be a green grocer.

Where do ghosts learn to read?
Elementary ghoul

CARY CANNIBAL AT A GLANCE

fave lunch:
Mac and Cheese

fave beverage:
Dr. Pepper

fave animal:
Aunt-eater

future job:
Waiter
(likes to serve people)

His mother:
Had a husband
and ate kids

Quote:
"lately, I'm fed up with people."

How is a small bucket like Dracula?
They're both a little pail.

**How did Quasimodo know which
football team would win?**
He didn't — he just had a hunch.

Why don't ghosts use pay phones?
They never have the right chains.

What did the ghost have on his computer?
A screamsaver

**If the Blob and the Thing were drowning, and you
could only save one of them, would you go to lunch
or play video games?**

How do you keep Godzilla from crashing your party?
Send him an invitation.

TWO-HEADED MONSTER, AT A GLANCE

fave gum:
Doublemint

fave dance:
Cha-cha

fave toy:
Yo-yo

fave place:
Bora-Bora

fave candy:
Bon-bons

Bad habit:
Double parking

Overheard remark:
"Did we like the movie?
Yes and no."

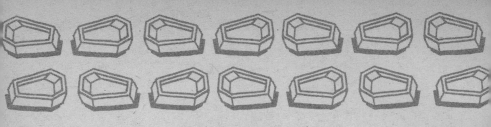

MONSTER KNOCK KNOCKS

KNOCK KNOCK
Who's there?

IVAN
Ivan who?

IVAN TO SUCK YOUR BLOOD!

KNOCK KNOCK
Who's there?

WITCH
Witch who?

WITCH YOU LET ME IN ALREADY?

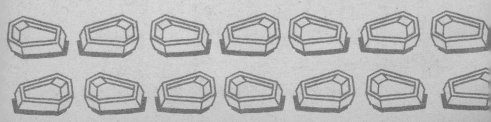

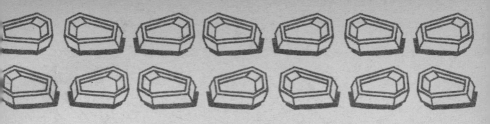

KNOCK KNOCK
Who's there?
KNOCK
Knock who?
KNOCK LESS MONSTER COMING TO VISIT!

KNOCK KNOCK
Who's there?
GHOST
Ghost who?
GHOST-AND IN THE CORNER!

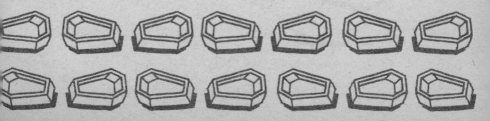

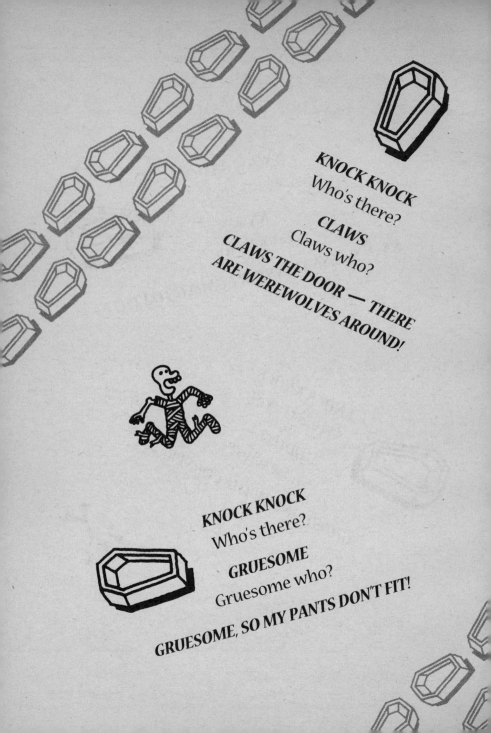

KNOCK KNOCK
Who's there?
CLAWS
Claws who?
**CLAWS THE DOOR — THERE
ARE WEREWOLVES AROUND!**

KNOCK KNOCK
Who's there?
GRUESOME
Gruesome who?
GRUESOME, SO MY PANTS DON'T FIT!

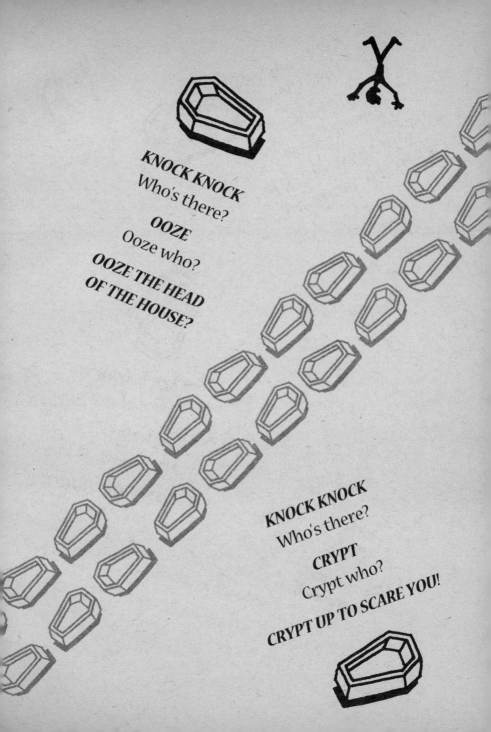

KNOCK KNOCK
Who's there?

OOZE
Ooze who?

**OOZE THE HEAD
OF THE HOUSE?**

KNOCK KNOCK
Who's there?

CRYPT
Crypt who?

CRYPT UP TO SCARE YOU!

KNOCK KNOCK
Who's there?

THUMPING
Thumping who?

**THUMPING BLACK IS
CRAWLING UP YOUR ARM!**

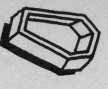

KNOCK KNOCK
Who's there?

WORM
Worm who?

**WORM IN THE HOUSE,
ISN'T IT?**

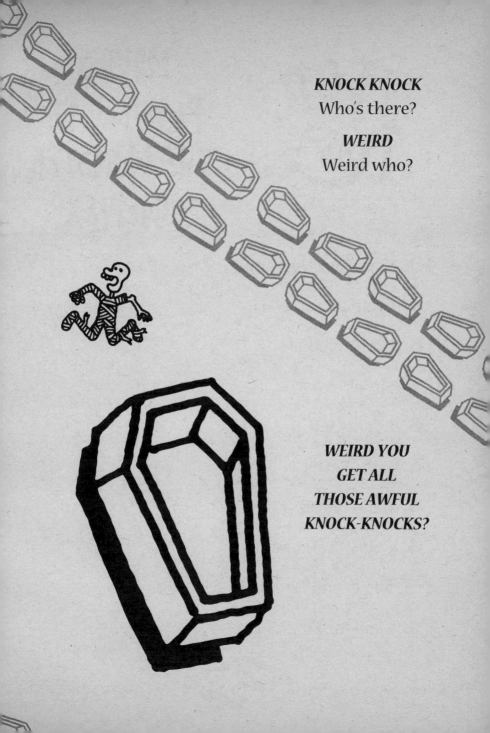

KNOCK KNOCK
Who's there?

WEIRD
Weird who?

**WEIRD YOU
GET ALL
THOSE AWFUL
KNOCK-KNOCKS?**

TOP 10 MOVIES PLAYING AT THE MONSTER CINEPLEX

10. Star Wars: The Vampire Strikes Back

9. Groundhag Day

8. Homely Alone 2

7. Shriek

6. Fright Club

5. Hairy Potter

4. Dude, Where's My Scar?

3. Good Will Haunting

2. Boo-ty and the Beast

1. Maul the King's Men

ARE YOU A

Take this quiz and find out.

1. You live in
   a. Michigan.
   b. Pennsylvania.
   c. Transylvania.

2. Your current fashion look:
   a. goth
   b. jock
   c. headwaiter

3. You do well in math because
   a. you study hard.
   b. you copy off Frankenstein.
   c. when you were little, your mother made you Count.

VAMPIRE?

4. You are repelled by
   a. piles of rat limbs.
   b. rotting maggot colonies.
   c. garlic.

5. After a long, hard day you like
to relax by
   a. doing a crossword puzzle.
   b. opening juice cans with your teeth.
   c. attacking villagers and watching
     "American Idol."

6. When you go to a Chinese restaurant,
you order
   a. cold sesame noodles.
   b. General Tso's chicken.
   c. General Tso.

7. A bully at school challenges you to a fight. You:

 a. say, "OK, but I barf when I'm nervous."

 b. pencil him in for June 2030.

 c. turn into a bat and fly away.

8. Another word for "oozing bloody flesh wound" is:

 a. boo-boo

 b. mutilation

 c. breakfast

9. You look around your room and see giant cobwebs, heaps of dust, and rotting animals. Do you

 a. appreciate how tidy it is?

 b. hire a cleaning service?

 c. ring the dinner bell?

10. Your favorite place to eat is

 a. Burger King.

 b. White Castle.

 c. your castle.

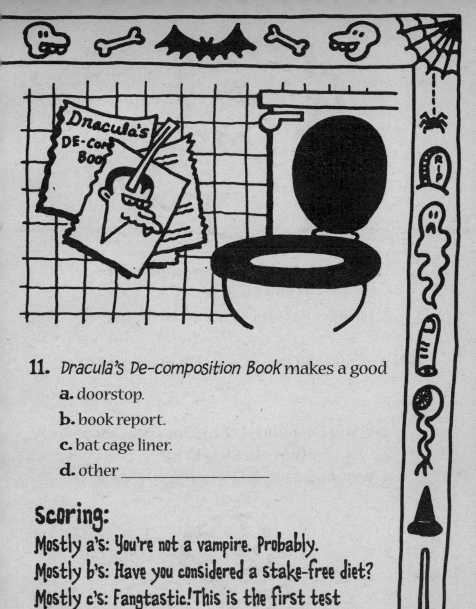

11. *Dracula's De-composition Book* makes a good

   a. doorstop.

   b. book report.

   c. bat cage liner.

   d. other _____

Scoring:

Mostly a's: You're not a vampire. Probably.

Mostly b's: Have you considered a stake-free diet?

Mostly c's: Fangtastic! This is the first test you've aced since 1763!

**Why did Dr. Frankenstein stop making
the monster?**
He didn't have the heart to keep going!

What grades did Dracula get on his report card?
20 cc's

**Did you hear about the giant cockroach
that ate Cleveland?**
Yeah, it's a nasty bug that's going around.

"THE MORGUE, THE MERRIER!"

Did you hear about the skinny vampire
who couldn't gain weight?
His eating was all in vein.

Why did the gravedigger write a book?
He had a good plot.

Did you hear about the cannibal
who resembled his parents?
He had his father's nose
and his mother's eyes.

CYCLOPS AT A GLANCE

fave restaurant:
Eye-hop

fave TV:
American Eye-dol

fave country:
Eye-ran

fave exercise machine:
The Staremaster

Quote:
"You're a sight for sore eye!"

**What did one tombstone say
to another?**
"Don't take me for granite."

Why did Dracula go to the World Series?
He heard they had baseball bats.

What did the ghost do when Dracula called?
Put him on shrieker phone.

**Why did the spirit
commute between
L.A. and N.Y.?**
He was bi-ghostal.

**Why did the ghost join
the army?**
So he could fright for his
country.

How do ghosts make extra money in the summer?
They moan lawns.

After visiting Alaska, why did Godzilla use ten bottles of shampoo?
He was trying to get the moose out of his hair.

What do you say when you meet a ghost?
"How do you boo?"

Why did the zombie have a bad time on his birthday?
'Cause no one was the life of the party.

Teacher: Caitlin, what's the difference between a man and Big Foot?
Caitlin: One is stupid, covered with matted hair, and smells awful. The other has big feet.

What do witches wear to bed?
Fright gowns

GARY GHOST
AT A GLANCE

fave luncheon meat:
Boo-logna

fave painting:
The Moaning Lisa

fave fluid:
Wite-Out

fave airline:
Scare France

Pet peeve:
Chain letters

fave ride:
Roller ghoster

Slogan:
"Just passing
through!"

Where do spirits buy stamps?
At the ghost office

How do you know the Invisible Man has no kids?
Because he's not apparent.

Why did the witch get a detention?
She cursed at the teacher.

**What disease does Dracula
take pills for?**
High blood pressure

Why did the skeleton go to the beach?
To get a skele-tan

What time is Dracula's dentist appointment?
Tooth hurty

What does Godzilla listen to in his car?
Stalk radio

What kind of horse does a ghost ride?
A nightmare

DEAR PRINCIPAL NORTON,

Please excuse Dracula's absince from school. He woke up pale and coffin, with a bad case of flew. He keeps asking ~~for~~ ~~throats~~ throat lozenges. Mrs. Crone must be mistakin about seeing him at the video arcade.

Signed,

~~My~~ Dracula's Mom

P.S. DON'T mention this when you see me. And <u>don't</u> <u>call</u>, because our phone is broken.

Why are zombie houses small?
There's no living room.

Why did Dracula go to the orthodontist?
To improve his bite

Why did Godzilla eat Tokyo instead of Cancun?
Mexican food gives him gas.

Why did the mummy cry when he saw the pyramids?
His home was in ruins.

**Why don't comedians perform
for zombies?**
They like a live audience.

Clerk: Do you want to pay cash for
this monster?
Frankenstein: No. I'll just charge it.

**Why did Dracula take
up photography?**
He likes to work in a darkroom.

Why was there no food left after the monster's party?

Because everybody was a goblin.

What do witches wear at the beach?
Suntan potion

Why did Godzilla eat the North Pole?
He wanted a frozen dinner.

BEST THINGS

ABOUT BEING A CYCLOPS

5. Eyeglass made
in half the time

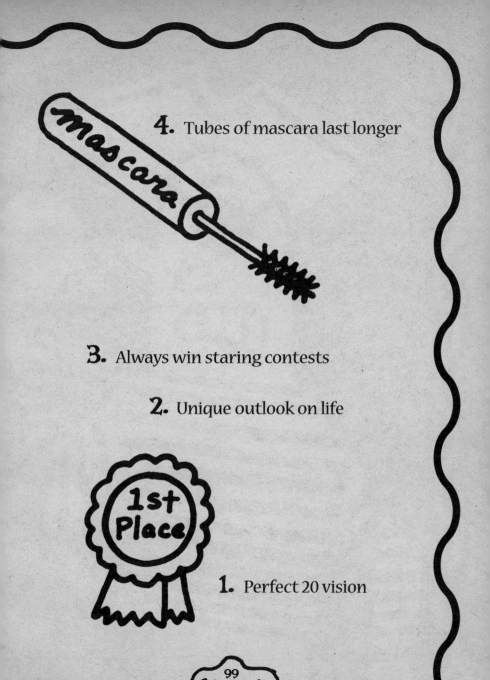

4. Tubes of mascara last longer

3. Always win staring contests

2. Unique outlook on life

1. Perfect 20 vision

WORST THINGS

ABOUT BEING A CYCLOPS

5. Can't wink

4. When angry, you lash out

3. Cornea sense of humor

2. "Pirate" eye-patch not advised

1. Forget teaching — you'll never have enough pupils

WHAT KIND OF MONSTER...?

Does tailoring on the side?
The abominable sew-man

Is brilliant and stitched together?
Frank Einstein

Is green, strong, and pouty?
The Incredible Sulk

Has one eye and bikes?
The cycle-ops

Has to clean up his room?
The Loch Mess Monster

Can be put in the dryer?
A wash 'n werewolf

Is a cowboy with a sore throat?
The headless hoarse man

Why does Frankenstein make a good gardener?
He has a green thumb.

**What do witches like to eat
in the summer?**
Ice-cream crones

**How can you tell if a werewolf's
been drinking from the toilet?**
His breath smells better.

**What football position does
the Blob play?**
Wide receiver

**Why do ghosts get kicked out of
movie theaters?**
They boo!

What do ghouls eat for dinner?
A five-corpse meal

How does a cremation guy get money?
He urns it.

What prize will the Blob never get?
The no-smell peace prize

Who comes to ghostly football games?
Spooktators

What did one maggot say to another?
"What's a nice girl like you doing in a joint like this?"

What happened to the witch's car?
It was toad.

CHAPTER 7

"JUST PULLING YOUR LEG OFF"

How did the undertaker get ready for the funeral?
He re-hearsed.

What kind of gum do ghosts chew?
Wrigley Fearmint

What do rich ghosts wear?
Satin sheets

Did you know that Godzilla has dandruff?
Yes, it's all over town.

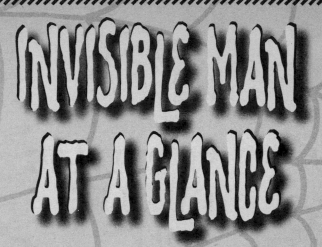

INVISIBLE MAN AT A GLANCE

fave music channel:
Empty-TV

fave cleanser:
Vanish

fave drink:
Evaporated milk

Pet peeve:
Teacher marking him absent

fave clothes:
See-through

Quote:
"Nice to not see you again!"

Why don't swamp monsters fly?
They can't get past airline security.

How do skeletons talk to each other?
By cell bone

What do mummies like for lunch?
A chicken wrap

Why can't Godzilla be on the radio?
He would break it.

Why does Dracula wear a black cape?
His blue one is at the cleaners.

What do monsters use to write with?
Ballpoint men

Does Dracula like to drive on back roads?
No, he prefers major arteries!

Why did Godzilla eat the U.S. Treasury when he was done with supper?
He wanted an after-dinner mint.

Music teacher: Your singing
is terrible!
Teen witch: Sorry, I've got
a frog in my throat.

What do you get when Godzilla sneezes?
Out of the way!

What do cannibals order at McDonald's?
The Kid's Meal

What do ghosts like in their coffee?
Non-dairy screamer

SKELETON AT A GLANCE

fave peanut butter:
Extra crunchy

fave toy:
Bony Playstation

fave store:
The Body Shop

fave chicken:
Skinless

Best feature:
High cheekbones

Slogan:
"No body does it better!"

DRACULA'S SPEED DIAL

#1 Bed, Bat, and Beyond

#2 Slurp-N-Save

#3 Frankenstein (cell)

#4 Bob's Funeral Home ("Free Delivery")

#5 Starbucks Coffins

#6 ~~Dr. Jekyll Mr Hyde Dr. Jekyll Mr Hyde~~
Dr. Jekyll

#7 Cute ghoul in math

#8 1-800-CASKETS

#9 Godzilla (home)

#10 Citibloodbank

Why did the baby Cyclops have so many holes in his head?
He was learning to eat with a fork.

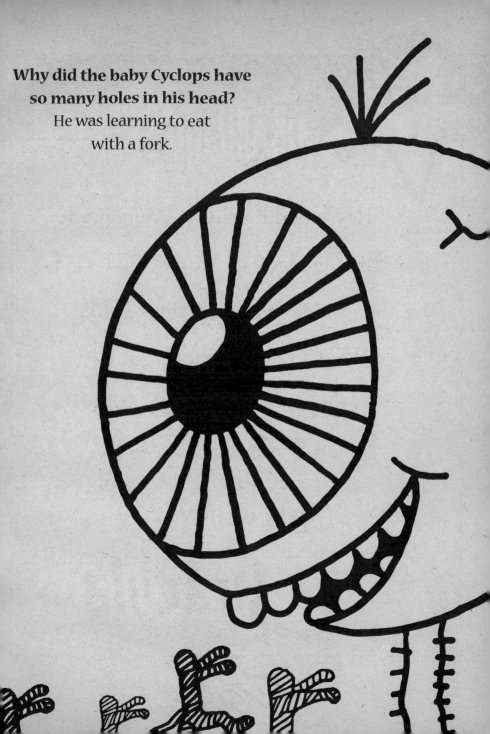

DRACU-BLOG

Hey blood brothers! Welcome to the bloodacious blog of Rad Vlad, Bludd Boi, Notorious R.I.P. Want to give a shout-out to my creeps: ZomB, Wanda Witch, God-Z: grave-robbin' 4-EVA!

Clots of love,

Dracula

What I Did Today

3/24. Got up and fed the bats.

On school bus, had all the seats to myself again.

Tried out for the school play, got a bit part.

My lab partner let me copy his homework — he's always sticking his neck out for me.

Right now, just hanging.

DRAC FAQS

Would you call yourself a type A personality?
I'm more of a type AB personality.

Is it true you like to suck your victims' blood, and
then put them in your hearse?
NO, I NEVER DRINK AND DRIVE.

During the summer, where do you go for fun?
To the beach! Give me a tube of 750 SPF
sunblock, and I'm there.

How do you get such good grades?
I pull all-nighters.

Innie or outie?
Outie this world!

FANG

FANG MAIL

Dracula — you rule and you GNAW it!

xoxo, Ashy

Hey, Bludd Boi, UR fierce. Piece out!

-Frankenstein

Let's party. I'll show you howl.

— Dr. Jekyll

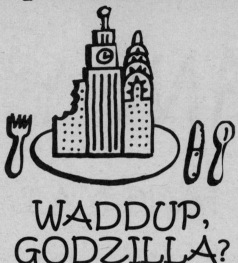

WADDUP, GODZILLA?

Godzilla has been writing online reviews of his meals.

Was in the mood for Chinese food, so I ate Hong Kong. It was good (burp).

— 'Zilla

Send a **Dracula e-Card** with your choice of messages:

Gon-drac-ulations!

Best Vicious!

Die, Monster, Die!

DRAC STATS

what I'm eating: (trans) Fusion cuisine

what I'm watching: "Primp My Coffin"

what I'm listening to: 80s bands (1780s)

CLASSIFIED VLADS

graveYARD SALE

People r dying to get in!
Bargains on tombstones, caskets, maggots.
Bring fiends.

Organ donor$ wanted

SteveSkeleton@hotmaul.com

Help wanted — Bob's Funeral Home

Need employees who can think
outside the box.
555-BURY

Bat-to-school Shopping? Try These!

The Drac-Pac

X-tra roomy backpack large enough to carry books, gym-cape, fang floss, and cadavers. Side pocket for blood bottle.

Dracula's "Sweatin' to the Oldies" Exorcise Video

Ten minutes a day to killer abs. Shake your boo-ty to (haunted) house music, techno, oldies, etc. Disco isn't dead!

Sun "B" Gone

Handy spray. May cause itching, boils, retching, foaming at the mouth — or your money back.

DRACU-BLOG

ASK DRACULA

Bat Advice

Dear Dracula,
I've been dating a guy for two weeks,
and I just found out he has a wooden leg.
What should I do?
— Confused

Dear Confused,
Break it off.

Dracula

Dear Dracula,
I've been looking everywhere for
a monster with one eye.
— Scar-lett Johansson

Dear Scar-lett,
Well, why don't you use two? (Duh).
Dracula

Dear Dracula,
My ghost boyfriend got lost in a fog.
What will happen to him?
— Courtney

Dear Courtney,
He'll be mist.
Dracula

Dear Dracula,
School just started and I don't like my teacher.
What should I do?
— Disappointed in Denver

Dear DD,
Maybe ketchup would help?
Dracula

Dear Dracula,
My mom is always getting on my case 'cuz I won't
wear a scarf. But I have a lovely neck, and I want
to show it off! Who's right?
— Tina in Teaneck

Dear Tina,
What's your address?
This needs to be answered in person—
Dracula

DRACU-BLOG

RECIPE KORNER

Ants on a Log

What you'll need: ants,
log, cream cheese.
Fill log with cheese and
ants. Eat log.

I-Scream Sundae

What you'll need:
two flavors of ice cream,
bananas, nuts,
hot sludge sauce.
Top with bloodshot
eyeball.

The Blob's Household Tips

Dusting As often as possible.
Use dandruff, crumbs, anything.

Bathing Twice a year with essential oils
(I like motor oil).
Lather, rinse, repeat.

Nutrition To tell if there are rat pieces
in your cookies, read the ingredients.

Laundry Pile clothes in washing machine;
set to "puree."

Wardrobe Always buy pants with
flies in them.

126

SPORTS SHORTS

 In the big game, the Zombies were ahead 8–5, until the Mummies tied things up.

The Ghosts kicked a field ghoul. Godzilla had two free throws . . . unfortunately, he threw them across the Grand Canyon.

The Blob fouled out, and the two-headed monster double dribbled.

DAILY HORROR-SCOPE

Aquarius: The 14th is *not* a good day to leave your casket.

Pisces: This month will bring lots of offers — from plastic surgeons.

Aries: Not having a nose doesn't mean you don't smell.

Taurus: Leave that cadaver alone. Some romances aren't meant to be.

Gemini: Chain yourself in a dungeon until sunrise.

Cancer: You'll be invited to a party six feet under. If you're in the mud, go!

Leo: Garbage monsters have trouble getting dates, but don't worry, someone will take you out.

Virgo: Don't eat prune pizza and then complain when you get pizzeria.

Libra: Today, you'll eat a handsome stranger. . . .

Scorpio: Don't blame yourself. The restaurant said they served children.

Sagittarius: You have the body of an Olympic athlete. Please give it back.

Capricorn: You are about to go on a trip. Tie your shoe laces.

How do werewolf presidents get around?
On Hair Force One

Did you hear that Dracula filed his fangs?
He wanted to make a point.

Where does a witch go to win prizes?
A warts ceremony

**What did the witch do when
she became the boss?**
She made sweeping changes.

Television announcer: Weather today is
swampy, with a chance of bugs . . .
Monster: Another perfect day!

Do zombies like being dead?
Of corpse!

Why do ghosts go around scaring people?
They're just trying to eeek out a living.

When do you find monsters at Yankee Stadium?
When there's a doubleheader.

What's a vampire's favorite period in history?
The Dark Ages

Where does a werewolf get a new tail?
At a re-tail store

How do werewolves greet each other?
Howl do you do?

What do hungry mummies do at hotels?
They call tomb service.

**What happened when the Blob appeared
on Broadway?**
There were lots of ooze and ahs.

How do you say yes to a Cyclops?
Eye-eye, sir!

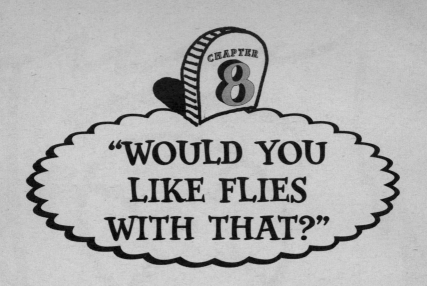

"WOULD YOU LIKE FLIES WITH THAT?"

What did Dracula do when the moat around his castle dried up?
He clicked the re-moat.

Why did it take both Frankenstein and Godzilla so long to help the little old lady across the street?
She didn't want to go!

Witch: Do you want your eyeball pie cut into six or eight slices?
Warlock: Make it six — I can't eat eight.

What music do witches like?
Hagtime

Why did the undertaker and his wife buy two cars?
One was his, one was hearse.

Ben: Did you watch the *Bride of Frankenstein* last night?
Sam: No, your sister had her shades drawn.

Bill: I've just been bitten by a vampire on one arm!
Jill: Which one?
Bill: I don't know. One vampire looks like another!

KING KONG AT A GLANCE

Fave TV show:
Chimp My Ride

Fave store:
Banana Republic

Fave activity:
Catching some
(chimpan)'Zs

Fave plane:
The Kongcorde

Fave hang-out:
Jungle gym

Seeks:
Gorilla his dreams

Slogan:
"Show me the monkey!"

How many witches does it take to change a lightbulb? Just one . . . but she changes it into a frog!

LIGHTBULB

JOKES

**How many Blobs does it take
to change a lightbulb?**
Two. One to hold the bulb in the socket,
one to rotate him.

**How many clean, well-dressed monsters
does it take to change a lightbulb?**
Both of them.

**How many vampires does it take
to change a lightbulb?**
Are you kidding? Vampires love the dark!

**How many wizards does it take
to change a lightbulb?**
It depends what you want to change it into.

**How many Godzillas does it take
to change a lightbulb?**
One to do it, seventeen to rebuild the house.

HEADLESS HORSEMAN AT A GLANCE

Goal:
To get a head

Pet peeve:
Drivers cutting
him off

fave jewelry:
Neck-less

fave store:
Hole Foods

Average grade:
Incomplete

Quote:
"You should see the other guy!"

Dracula's TOP 10 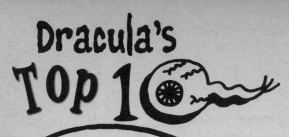 No-Fail Homework Excuses

10. My **werewolf** ate it.

9. I gave it to the Invisible Man, and he **disappeared.**

8. Godzilla used it for **TP.**

7. I was busy with the school **blood drive.**

6. It fell through a **time warp** — I handed it in five years ago.

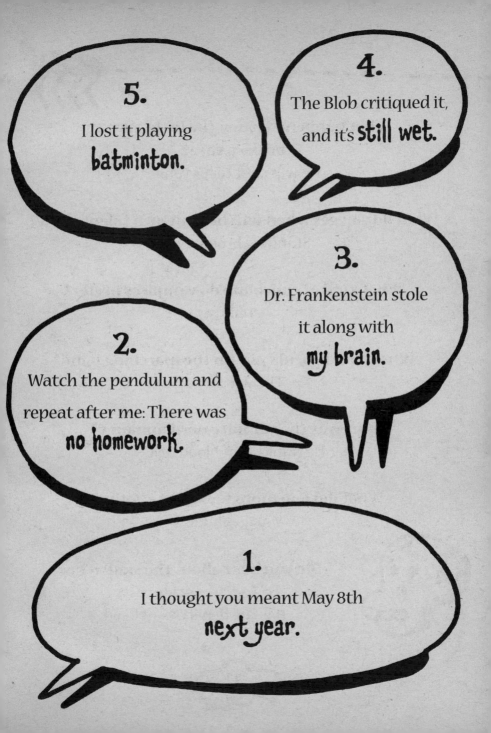

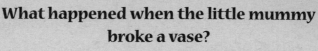

What happened when the little mummy broke a vase?
He was sent to his tomb.

What do you get when witches put on a talent show?
Standing broom only

What kind of chocolate do vampires prefer?
Dark!

What does Dracula play in the marching band?
The windpipe

Why was the vampire nerd unhappy?
He flunked his blood test.

What did one monster say to another?
"You go, ghoul!"

Did you hear about the skull who teaches science?
He's the department head.

144

MONSTER MIDDLE SCHOOL

Est. 1932

"We Mold Young Minds, Lungs, and Kidneys"

REPORT CARD

Dracula, Count GRADE **7**

SUBJECT	GRADE
MATH	D
ENGLISH	D-
HISTORY	D+
SCIENCE	F+
PHYS ED	F

Chews gum (and flesh) in class.
Always asking to go to the bat room.

SUSPENDED

99% of Vampires Give the rest of US a bad name
Go Green
GODZILLA IS MY CO-PILOT
GIVE BLOOD
HANG IN THERE!

**How did the ghost teach her students
to go through a wall?**
She went through it again and again.

Loch Ness Monster: Do you like barnacles?
Swamp Thing: They're growing on me.

When do monsters usually appear?
Just before someone screams

**Why did King Kong climb up the Empire
State Building?**
He didn't fit in the elevator.

Did you hear about the cannibal who ate his sibling?
Now he's got a half-brother.

**Why did Swamp Thing grow legs and walk
out of the sea?**
He had to go to the bathroom.

Cannibal mother: Why don't you eat that bratty kid?
Cannibal son: He's spoiled!

Why did the cannibal go on Wheel of Fortune?
To buy a bowel

Where do ghosts shop?
Chain stores

"BECAUSE I'M THE MUMMY, THAT'S WHY."

Why did the princess marry the ghost?
He was very haunt-some.

What do you get when there are too many werewolves around?
Claws-trophobia

What do you serve a witch for dinner?
A twelve-curse meal

Why did the zombie turn down an offer to dance?
He was undead on his feet.

Why did the monster knit her son three socks?
Because he grew another foot.

What kind of ghosts do you find on airplanes?
Fright attendants

Executioner #1: What are you doing tonight?
Executioner #2: Just hanging.

Cross-eyed monster: When I grow up, I want to be
a bus driver.
Dracula: Well, I won't stand in your way.

Why did Godzilla take two weeks to finish a book?
He wasn't very hungry.

TOP 10

MONSTER ICE BREAKERS

10. What's a nice gargoyle like you doing in a place like this?

9. I'd ask you to dance, but I've got four left feet.

8. You've certainly got the figure for that witch's robe!

7. Haven't I drooled on you somewhere before?

6. Excuse me, would you brush the worms out of my back hair?

5. You are drop-dead stunning!

4. I'd like to wrap my 24 arms around you.

3. Great alligator shoes. Oh — you're barefoot!

2. We see eye to eye to eye.

1. Kiss me, I'm slimy.

IT'S RHYME FOR A JOKE

What do you call . . . ?

A two-headed instructor?
Creature teacher

A torturer who keeps a web journal?
A blogger flogger

A sky raining Godzillas?
A lizard blizzard

What ghouls eat with jam?
Ghost toast

A popular cemetery plot?
Fave grave

A chewy Nefertiti?
A gummy mummy

A witch's purse?
A hag bag

A skeleton horse?
A bony pony

A vampire Godzilla steps on?
A flat bat

A friendly Egyptian tomb-dweller?
A chummy mummy

What you got from Rent-A-Monster?
A leased beast

Monster spit?
Ghoul drool

The Blob and the Thing?
A gruesome twosome

A grave-robbing pirate?
A demon seaman

A group of teen vampires?
A fang gang

**What did the zombie mother say
to her son the corpse?**
Where in earth have you been?

**What time is it when Dracula, Godzilla,
Frankenstein, the Blob, and the Abominable
Snowman are chasing a witch?**
Five after one

MONSTER ANSWERING MACHINE MESSAGES

From a mummy:
"I can't come to the phone now because I'm tied up. . . ."

From the Blob:
"Leave a message at the sound of the creep. . . ."

From Dracula:
"At the tomb, leave your name, address, and blood type. . . ."

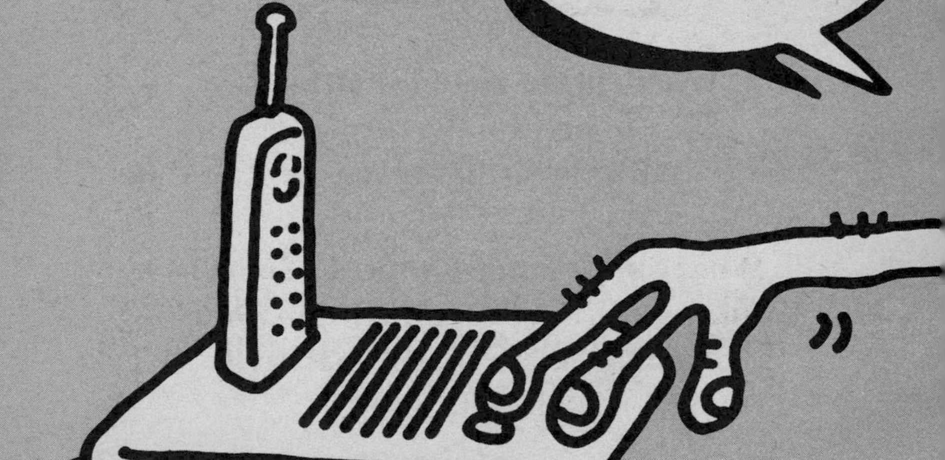

What do mummies talk about?
Old times

Why don't people allow werewolves in their houses?
They shed on the couch.

**Why did Godzilla eat Chicago, skip over Cleveland,
and then eat Detroit?**
He didn't want to eat between meals!

**Why did the five hundred pound, slobbering,
three-headed monster stay out of the sun?**
She didn't want to ruin her looks.

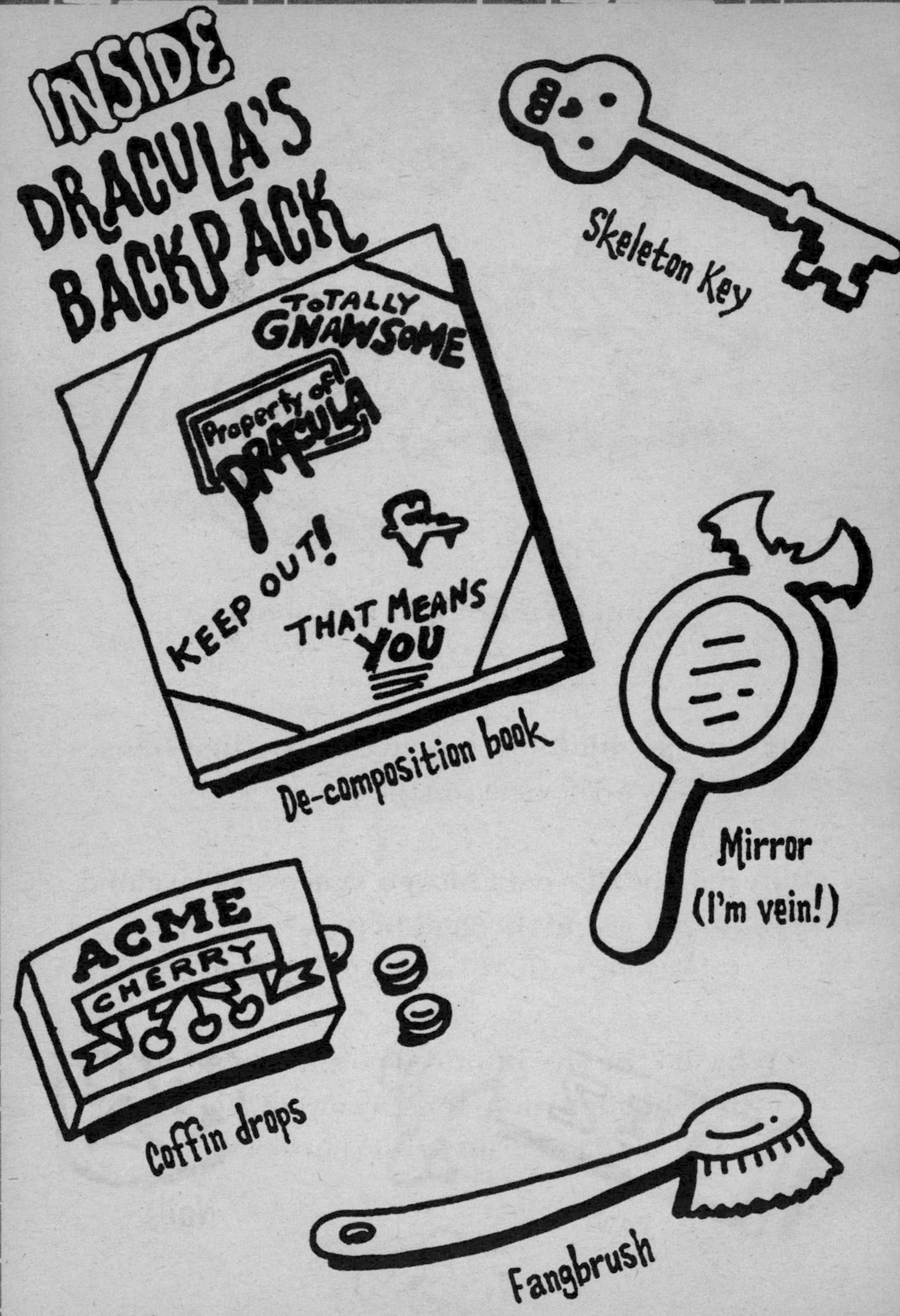
INSIDE DRACULA'S BACKPACK
TOTALLY GNAWSOME
Property of DRACULA
KEEP OUT!
THAT MEANS YOU
De-composition book
Skeleton Key
Mirror
(I'm vein!)
ACME
CHERRY
Coffin drops
Fangbrush

Witch watch

Cell phone

Juice

Candy

Nails
(must stop biting)

Why did the ghost hire a maid?
He wanted someone to change his sheets.

**What's the last thing to go through Dracula's mind
as he crashes into a window?**
His rear end

Why did the zombie get kicked out of school?
He had lousy graves.

Why did the traffic cop arrest the mummy?
He was going 80 Niles-per-hour.

How did the two-headed monster win the relay race?
He had a head start.

**What did the police do when Godzilla took the
highway to town?**
They made him put it back.

Why was the Invisible Man sad?
His girlfriend said she couldn't see him anymore.

What does a werewolf do if a spark falls on him?
He calls the fur department.

I'LL ALWAYS DISMEMBER YOU

Yearbook Signings at Monster Middle School

WHEN I miss you,
I'll think again,
Of your teeth in my neck
at 9 am.
— Tiffany Jones

from the two-headed monster
Steven and Seth
Who always know
If they have bad breath.

Dracula,
Would i have gotten
2 know u better
if i hadn't worn
turtleneck sweaters?
— Ghoulia G.

IM or call,
to me it's the same.
Just don't ask
for my SCREAM name.
— Zeke Zombie

To my BFF,
I'll always B true
Too bad I'll never
Be there 4 u.
— Invisible Man

FaNGS for the memories!!! - Mr. Hyde

Drac,
You're the best friend
I ever made
in fifty years
of seventh grade.
- Vampirella

This year I've
enjoyed
getting to gnaw
you
- Loch Ness
Monster

Congratulations on the
grads-u-ate!
- Godzilla

Eating lunch was fun —
Your mom sure makes a
great hamburger!
— Cary Cannibal

Blood is red,

Flesh is rotten. . . .

Sorry, that's as far as I got.

— Wanda Witch

**If ONLY I
were good at art
I'd use this
space
TO DRAW A FART.**
— THE BLOB

Why don't girls like Dracula?
He has bat breath.

Why did the Blob cross the road?
To get to the odor side.

Why go to a monster for advice?
Because four heads are better than one.

Igor: How's your job gluing bodies together?
Frankenstein: Fast paste.

**What do undertakers get
at football games?**
Box seats!

**Did you hear the Blob lost
his job as a chauffeur?**
He was driving away
customers.

**Why couldn't Godzilla
cross the road?**
The traffic was
too heavy.

**What did Dracula
require from his
computer?**
More mega-bytes

**Why was the cannibal
kicked out of class?**
For buttering up the
teacher

What did Dracula say when he finished this book?

"Bat's all, folks!"

170